Oonga Boonga

Frieda Wishinsky Michael Martchenko

Scholastic Canada Ltd.

Toronto   New York   London Auckland Sydney
Mexico City New Delhi Hong Kong Buenos Aires

The illustrations in this book were painted in watercolour
on Crescent Illustration Board.

This book was designed in QuarkXPress, with type set in
22 point Stempel Schneidler.

Scholastic Canada Ltd.
604 King Street West, Toronto, Ontario M5V 1E1, Canada

Scholastic Inc.
557 Broadway, New York, NY 10012, USA

Scholastic Australia Pty Limited
PO Box 579, Gosford, NSW 2250, Australia

Scholastic New Zealand Limited
Private Bag 94407, Greenmount, Auckland, New Zealand

Scholastic Children's Books
Euston House, 24 Eversholt Street, London NW1 1DB, UK

Library and Archives Canada Cataloguing in Publication
Wishinsky, Frieda
Oonga boonga / Frieda Wishinsky ; illustrated by Michael Martchenko.

ISBN 978-1-4431-0773-0

I. Martchenko, Michael II. Title.

PS8595.I834O6 2011   jC813'.54   C2010-907359-2

8 7 6 5 4 3 2 1   Printed in Singapore   46   11 12 13 14

Nobody could make
Baby Louise stop crying.

Her mother tried. She held her close
and sang a little lullaby.

But that didn't help.

Louise kept on crying till her tears
ran like rivers to the sea.

Her father tried. He rocked her gently in his arms and whispered softly in her ear.

But that didn't help.

Louise kept on crying till her wails shook the pictures off the walls.

Grandma tried. She gave her
a nice warm bottle and said, "Eat. Eat."
But that didn't help.
Louise kept on crying till her sobs
woke all the dogs and cats on the block.

Grandpa tried. He played a happy tune
on his harmonica and did a little jig.
But that didn't help.

Louise kept on crying till the birds
flew out of the trees and the squirrels
scampered away.

The neighbors came and offered advice.
"Turn her on her stomach."
"Turn her on her back."
"Change her diaper."

"Play Mozart."
"Play rock and roll."
But nothing helped.

Louise kept on crying.

Then her brother, Daniel, came home from school.

"Oonga Boonga," he said to Louise.

Louise looked up, tears still streaming down her face.

"Oonga Boonga," he repeated.
Louise stopped sobbing and
looked him straight in the eye.
"Oonga Boonga," said Daniel again.
Louise broke into a smile.

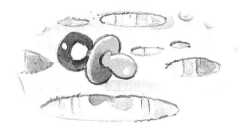

"How did you do that?" asked his mother.
"It's easy. You just say Oonga Boonga,"
said Daniel.

"Oonga Boonga," said his mother.

"Oonga Boonga," said his father.

"Oonga Boonga," said Grandma and Grandpa.

"See," said Daniel, "she likes it."

And sure enough, she did.
Louise was smiling from ear to ear.
"Oonga Boonga," said everyone
in unison.

"I'm going out to play," said Daniel.

"Be back at six for dinner," said his mom.

But as soon as he left, Louise's smile faded. Slowly a tear rolled down her cheek, followed by another, and then another.

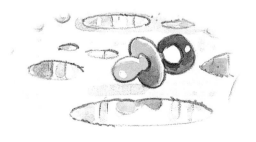

Soon she was crying as loudly as before.

"Oonga Boonga," said her mother.

"Oonga Boonga," said her father.

"Oonga Boonga," said Grandma and Grandpa.

But nothing helped. Louise kept on crying.

"I think she wants Daniel,"
said her mother.

"Here I am," said Daniel.

Then he leaned over and
whispered,

"Bonka Wonka, Louise."

And to no one's surprise, Louise stopped crying.